sleepover Girls

Sleepover Girls is published by Capstone Young Readers
A Capstone Imprint
1710 Roe Crest Drive
North Mankato, Minnesota 56003
www.capstoneyoungreaders.com

Library of Congress Cataloging-in-Publication Data is available on the Library of Congress website.
ISBN: 978-1-62370-193-2 (paperback)
ISBN: 978-1-4342-9755-6 (library binding)
ISBN: 978-1-4342-9763-1 (eBook)

Summary: The Sleepover Girls just found out some MAJOR news. Teen pop star Luke Lewis is returning to his — and their — hometown of Valley View to hold a special benefit concert. To top it off, the local radio station is having a contest and the winner gets to meet Luke! Maren is Luke's biggest fan and is dead set on winning the contest. The challenge? Create a love letter to Valley View showing your hometown pride. Maren wastes no time enlisting the Sleepover Girls' help to make the most awesome scrapbook ever. Will her project hit the right note or fall flat?

Designed by Tracy McCabe

Illustrated by Paula Franco

Printed in China by Nordica
0414/CA21400619
032014 008095NORDF14

Maren Loves Luke Lewis

by Jen Jones

capstone young readers

Maren Melissa Taylor

Maren is what you'd call "personality-plus" – sassy, bursting with energy, and always ready with a sharp one-liner. She dreams of becoming an actress or comedienne one day and moving to Hollywood to make it big. Not one to fuss over fashion, you'll often catch Maren wearing a hoodie over a sports tee and jeans. She is an only child, so she has adopted her friends as sisters.

Willow Marie Keys

Patient and kind, Willow is a wonderful confidante and friend. (Just ask her twin, Winston!) She is also a budding artist with creativity for miles. She will definitely own her own store one day, selling everything she makes. Growing up in a hippie-esque family, Willow acquired a Bohemian style that perfectly suits her flower child within.

Delaney Ann Brand

Delaney's smart and motivated – and she's always on the go! Whether she's volunteering at the animal shelter or helping Maren with her homework, you can always count on Delaney. You'll usually spot low-maintenance Delaney in a ponytail and jeans (and don't forget her special charm bracelet, with unique charms to symbolize each one of the Sleepover Girls). She is a great role model for her younger sister, Gigi.

Ashley Francesca Maggio

Ashley is the baby of a lively Italian family. Her older siblings (Josie, Roman, Gino, and Matt) have taught her a lot, including how to get attention in such a big family, which Ashley has become a pro at. This fashionista-turned-blogger is on top of every style trend and shares it with the world via her blog, Magstar. Vivacious and mischievous, Ashley is rarely sighted without her beloved "purse puppy," Coco.

chapter One

My mom's giant Dr. Seuss hat came around the corner before she did. My mom sure knows how to make me smile.

"Happy half birthday, Mare-Bear!" she said, tilting the cake so the four of us could see her proud creation.

Since it was only half a cake, it was easy to see the bright rainbow layers in all of their glory—chocolate, red velvet, and vanilla. Pretty impressive for my mom, who is, as they say, a bit "domestically challenged" in the kitchen. On top of the cake, a star-shaped candle shone brightly atop cursive text that read simply, "Maren's a Star!"

Ashley stood up and started waving her hands as if conducting an imaginary orchestra. "Happy . . ."

"HALF!" Delaney and Willow shouted, giggling at the nerdiness of it all.

". . . birthday to you. Happy (HALF!) birthday to you. Happy (HALF!) birthday, dear Maren. Happy (HALF!) birthday to you!" As everyone finished the song and clapped, I had to smile. Although super cheesy, it was a memorable moment.

"Make a wish, Maren!" Willow urged, tucking a lock of long blond hair behind her ear. "Maybe it will come true."

"Well, that's easy," I replied, grinning. "I wish to become Mrs. Luke Lewis and have him serenade me every day and night for the rest of my life."

"You can't say your wish out loud or it won't come true," said Delaney.

"I don't care. It's worth saying Mrs. Luke Lewis out loud," I said dreamily.

Pursing my lips, I leaned forward and blew out the candle with a flourish. The girls laughed, and my mom rolled her eyes.

If you're wondering who Luke Lewis is, you obviously haven't listened to the radio or watched YouTube or looked at any popular magazines in, oh, forever.

Luke Lewis is the most amazing guitar-toting, hipster-haired pop singer of all time. And the coolest thing? Luke actually grew up in Valley View, our hometown! Yep, he even went to the same middle school we attend. I like to pretend my desk was his back in the day. Hey, a girl can dream.

"How about you finish sixth grade before you run off to marry a pop star?" said my mom good-naturedly. She grabbed the cake so she could go cut it in the kitchen.

"Ahh, that reminds me," said Ash, reaching into her oversized striped tote. "This may not be as good as a marriage license, but I have something for you."

She handed me a small rectangular package wrapped in polka-dot paper. After I eagerly tore it open, I couldn't help but laugh at what was inside. It was a framed magnetic photo of me and Luke Lewis! She'd taken a pic from our school dance and Photoshopped my body next to his in a red carpet photo.

"Ash, this is amazing!" I said, holding it up to my chest so Delaney and Willow could see. "This will make the perfect finishing touch for my locker. Or should we start calling it my Luke-r?"

Ashley giggled at my bad joke. "Roman helped me Photoshop it," she said. "I guess having a bunch of older brothers *does* come in handy sometimes."

Ash was one of five kids in a big Italian family; since her sister Josie was off at college, she was the only girl in her house. For such a girly girl, it was often boy overload for Ashley. But, like she said, there were plenty of perks, too, including meeting older boys.

"My turn," said Willow, handing me a gift bag with a swirly "M" on the outside. I had no doubt she'd stenciled it herself. The girl was so crafty. It always impressed me.

I opened the bag to unveil a chevron-patterned, hand-knit iPad cozy. But before I could admire it, Ashley snatched it from my hand.

"Are you kidding me?" she exclaimed. "Wills, this is above and beyond. You have to make me one for my birthday. Or half birthday. Or just for any day."

It really was above and beyond, but I'd learned not to expect anything less from Willow. She blushed as I gave her a hug. "Thanks, chiquita," I told her. "You rock! My iPad is going to be better dressed than me!"

It was Delaney's turn. She seemed a bit embarrassed. "Well, this pales in comparison, but here you go!"

She pulled a box from her own bag and handed it to me. "Sorry I didn't have time to wrap it. I was at the animal shelter all day." Delaney was a regular volunteer at Valley View Animal Rescue, which is where she had actually found her adorable dog, Frisco. Frisco could turn any person into a dog lover!

A closer look at the box revealed that it was actually a board game. I loved board games, so this was perfect!

"Oooh, Say Anything," I said, reading the label. "I should be good at that." It was no secret that I wasn't afraid to speak my mind!

"Yeah, we should definitely play later," said Ashley. "But not before cake!" I followed her gaze to the patio door, where my mom was coming out with slices of rainbow cake for all of us.

"You guys, thank you so much. You totally didn't have to get me gifts — it's not even my real birthday. Having you sleep over is more than enough."

And it was. Our weekly sleepovers had become the thing that got me through the school day on Friday — scratch that, the thing I looked forward to most every week!

On the rare occasion that we couldn't have our Friday sleepover, I was known to be a little crabby. (You can ask my mom.) Our sleepovers had earned us the nickname "The Sleepover

Girls" at school. It was definitely a fitting name for our fierce foursome.

The funny thing was that our sleepovers had started all because of me, in a way. My mom is the editor-in-chief of a travel mag called *Fly Girls*, and she's jet-setting much of the time for her job. (Sometimes I get to go with her! I'll never forget our South African safari.) Since she is gone a lot, Delaney's mom started watching me on weekends sometimes, and the two of us always had a blast. When my mom later returned the favor, Willow and Ashley joined in the fun. From there, the Sleepover Girls were born!

Even funnier was the fact that the half-birthday tradition had started because of my mom's job, too. Every year, her magazine hosts a big travel writing conference in New York City. It just happens to fall on the same weekend as my birthday. (I know, bummer, right?) Luckily, it's become an excuse to go visit my dad down in San Diego. A California birthday? Yes, please, says this Oregon girl.

So now I get to spend half birthdays with my mom, and my actual birthday with my dad and stepfamily. Of course, I'd rather that my parents were still together, but what are ya gonna do? At least my stepfamily is cool, and both my parents seem a lot happier now than they did when they were married.

As if on cue, my mom bent down and kissed the top of my head. "Love you, Red," she said, tousling my curly fire-red hair and pulling a hot pink envelope from her pocket. "You know I couldn't resist just one more half-birthday surprise."

Say what? We'd already done a manicure day earlier this week, plus the cake and sleepover. As usual, my mom had gone overboard. But I'm never one to turn down a gift! I ripped open the envelope and almost lost my breath when I saw what was inside.

"No you *didn't!*" I gasped, as my mood went from an already-high ten to off the charts. In front of me was a set of shiny Luke Lewis concert tickets to his *totally sold-out* show. The one I'd spent a whole afternoon on Ticketmaster trying to get. The one I'd called in trying to win radio giveaways a million times with no luck. I held the tickets up in the air, fanning them out so the girls could see, too. We all started jumping up and down and screaming.

"Ms. Taylor, you are my favorite person in life!" yelled Ashley, giving her a squeeze. My mom grinned. "I couldn't let Luke Lewis come back to Valley View and not help you girls get in on the fun," she said.

Blown away, I lifted my fizzy passion fruit drink to signify a toast. "This calls for a serious shout-out," I said, beaming at my mom. "To my awesome mom, and to another great *half* birthday that's been a *whole* lotta fun."

Maybe Luke Lewis wasn't my husband (yet), but getting to see him sing in person was second best. And as we all clinked glasses, I knew deep down that having the best BFFs ever made my life more than complete!

chapter Two

Okay, spoiler alert: I would much rather spend an afternoon curled up watching anything on the E! network than studying (who wouldn't?) School has never been my "thing" — much to my mom's dismay. Because I have a mild case of ADHD, it's pretty easy for me to lose focus when it's study time. So I wasn't at all surprised when my mom invited Delaney to stay after our sleepover for an impromptu study session. (After all, two heads are better than one, right?)

"Truth time, Maren. How far have you gotten in the book?" asked Delaney, flopping onto my bright blue beanbag to join me. "I think Mrs. Wynne wants us to read up to chapter six before the quiz this week."

I rolled my eyes and hid my face behind my book. "Does it count if I say I made it past the table of contents? It was fascinating."

Delaney swatted me playfully. "I don't think that's going to help you master any of the questions. C'mon, Mare! This book is actually good — pinky swear."

"That's easy for you to say," I groaned. "You *love* dogs, not to mention the fact that you're crazy smart."

"But you knew how serious I am about making a pinky swear, right? I wouldn't say it if it wasn't true," Delaney said seriously.

I knew how serious Delaney was about pinky promises, and I knew she wouldn't lie to me.

However, our assigned book was *Where the Red Fern Grows,* which is about a young boy who bonds with his two hunting dogs. As our resident dog fanatic, Delaney was sure to love this book. I wasn't quite as excited. In fact, I could barely get through the paragraph on the back cover let alone finish an entire chapter! This was not an easy assignment.

Delaney knew how to deal with me. "Well, why don't we try reading the first chapter out loud? That will help you absorb the info better, and I can help you if you get stuck," she suggested. It was pretty obvious that my mom had talked to her.

The only thing I hated more than reading to myself was reading out loud, and Delaney knew it. But deep down, I knew she was right. I put on my nerd-chic reading glasses for effect and grabbed the book out of Delaney's hands. I would do this, but I didn't have to like it.

It took what felt like forever to get through the first chapter, but somehow I managed to make it through. I could see why the story is a classic — it's a real page-turner! Delaney wasn't lying! As we started to slog through the second chapter, though, I felt the familiar restlessness creep in. Even with a good book, it was hard to stay focused.

"Laney, let's take a break," I said. "Willow dragged me to her tae kwon do class yesterday, and I'm already *so* sore. Sitting in one spot is just making it worse. I need to move, move, move!"

"Okay, ten minutes," she allowed. "But I'm going to have to go in a bit. My mom will kill me if I'm not home to walk Frisco soon." One of the conditions of Delaney adopting Frisco was that she had to be responsible for taking care of him, and Delaney took it super seriously. That Frisco was one lucky pup!

"Copy that," I said, bouncing up. "And I know the perfect way to burn some energy. Dance party!"

I turned on my radio and cranked the music. I started dancing around like a maniac to release my pent-up boredom, but Delaney just looked at me like I was a crazy person. By the end of the song, though, I broke her down and we were both grooving out! She helps me with homework, and I help her relax. Nothing beats a good dance party.

"Thanks for listening to Portland's 100.7 MOVE-FM," said the DJ once the song was over. "Next up, we've got Valley View's very own Luke Lewis. He'll be coming to town next month, and *you* could win a chance to meet him. Yes, you. Go to our website and get all the details right now."

"Um, are you *kidding* me?" I asked Delaney. "He did not just say that."

"He *so* did," said Delaney, grinning ear to ear. She turned up the volume on the radio so we could hear the Luke song better. I've learned that the music can never be too loud when a Luke song is on. My mom tends to disagree, but that usually doesn't stop me.

"Not only do we have tickets to his show, which is completely crazy, but we could *meet* him! I would just die. Commence Operation Mrs. Lewis," I said, pulling my iPad out of Willow's cute cozy. My new mission in life was winning this contest! (Besides finishing *Where the Red Fern Grows*, of course, in case my mom is reading this.)

I eagerly typed in the URL for the radio station and found all the need-to-know scoop on the home page. At Luke's concert, the mayor would be presenting him with a key to the city. The winner would get to be on stage and help present the key, too! Um, sign me up.

The spin of the contest involved submitting a "Love Letter to Valley View," and the most creative entry would win. We only had two weeks to finish the project. My wheels were already turning — a song? A poem? A photo essay? There are so many options!

Meeting Luke Lewis is my main focus in life, so this was serious business. I had to win this contest!

"What should we do? We need to think of something fast and get started," I said to Delaney. "I could write a love letter to Luke in my sleep, but a Love Letter to Valley View needs some serious thought."

"I hate to be lame, but you know we're getting totally off track, right?" she asked, tapping her finger on the book.

"Are you serious? I can't concentrate at a time like this!" I replied. "All of my dreams could come true with one contest."

"Good point," Delaney said. "I guess we are done studying for now." She probably knew there was no going back now that the "L" word had come up.

We racked our brains for a few minutes, but nothing seemed quite right. We talked about changing the lyrics from one of Luke's songs to be about Valley View and filming it for YouTube, but that seemed too obvious. Plus, we were all pretty bad singers. We wouldn't be able to give a Luke song the justice it deserved. This was harder than I thought.

"I've got it!" cried Delaney. I could almost see the lightbulb appear above her head. "Why don't we make a scrapbook? That would allow us to include lots of different things, and it would be obvious that we put tons of work into it. And you know Willow will be *all* over that."

"Bam!" I said. "I love that idea. Plus it's something we can all work on together, which makes it even more amazing. Looks like my dreams of becoming Mrs. Luke Lewis might just become a reality after all."

"May the best love letter win, and by that, I mean ours," she said.

chapter Three

In history class the next day, I found myself staring at the clock nonstop — and for once it had nothing to do with my ADHD. I was simply antsy to get to lunch, where an emergency brainstorming session had been called. It was time for the Sleepover Girls to get serious about Operation Mrs. Lewis.

When the bell finally rang, I sprang from my seat, almost knocking over my classmate Zoey in the process.

"Watch it!" she huffed, shooting me a death stare. "Are you really *that* hungry?"

Did I mention Zoey's not so friendly? We call her and her twin Franny the "Prickly Pair" for good reason. Sitting behind her every day during history is just about the worst thing ever.

I couldn't be bothered to go toe-to-toe with her this time, though. So I just rolled my eyes to let her know I wasn't fazed and kept going. After all, I had much more important plans. Ashley was waiting for me by the pizza station when I got to the cafeteria.

"Delaney and Willow are saving a table over there," she said, pointing to an area in the corner. I couldn't wait to grab some pizza and go sit with them.

But no sooner had Ashley and I filled our trays when a slice of bread came flying through the air and landed on mine. The loud laughter coming from a nearby table left no doubt as to who threw it. My "favorite" classmate, Chase Davis.

"Now you can be gingerbread, Maren," he yelled across the cafeteria. "Get it?"

I felt my cheeks turn red. I'm sure they were so red that they practically matched my ginger hair! I tossed the bread back to their table.

"You are so original," I replied. I turned my back so he couldn't get to me anymore, though my face was still on fire.

Ashley giggled. "Ahh, young love," she joked. "You know boys only tease the girls they like." My mom was always saying the same thing.

"Well then, Chase must be head over heels in love with me since he's constantly torturing me!" I complained.

My friends loved to tease me about Chase. They thought we were destined to be together and that he, well, "liked" me with a capital

"L." But what they refused to accept was that the thought of having a boyfriend was not at all appealing to me! (Well, unless it was Luke Lewis. But otherwise, no.)

We were all kind of at different "boy crazy" stages. Ash was a full-on flirt, Delaney had crushes here and there, and Willow thought boys were cute but was too shy to ever do anything about it. I was somewhere between everyone in the boy department, which suited me just fine.

It was just one more reminder of how different we all were. There was ever-fashionable Ash, clad in an impossibly cute cashmere cardigan, chunky necklace, and skinny jeans. Hippie chick Willow was wearing a long paisley maxi dress that made her look even taller, as if that was possible! Practical, ponytailed Delaney was keeping it simple in a V-neck and denim skirt. And I, of course, was rocking my Portland Trail

Blazers hoodie like a champ. (A shortage of sports clothing was *not* among my problems!)

Even our ideas for the "Love Letter to Valley View" were all over the map. "What if we do still pics from one of those time-lapse videos?" asked Delaney. "We could show all the people and cool things that happen on Main Street over 24 hours."

That seemed like a great idea, but none of us really knew how to do that or what kind of equipment we'd need.

"Love that, Laney, but pretty sure a Flip cam isn't going to cut it for something that high-tech," I told her. "Plus, remember, the scrapbook has to have different types of visuals: pics, artwork, and crafty stuff like that."

All of us looked at Willow at the same time. "I'm thinking! I'm thinking!" she said, taking a bite of her kale salad. She always brought her own healthy lunch, which was impressive.

"Picasso didn't create his masterpieces overnight."

Ashley's eyes lit up. "What if we find residents of all ages and backgrounds, and each person wears a shirt with one letter of the word 'Valley View?' It would show how diverse our small town is," suggested Ash.

It was just like Ashley to stage some sort of modeling shoot, but it was an awesome idea. Doing a photo like that would definitely show all of the different types of people who lived in Valley View.

"Now you've got your designer thinking cap on," I encouraged her, jotting the idea down in my notebook. "What else?"

Willow chimed in. "We should definitely take pics of all of the town landmarks," she said. "I could also draw fake postcards on those pages to jazz it up!" She jotted down a quick diagram of what she was picturing on a napkin. We all nodded excitedly, impressed by what she could create in just seconds.

"Love it!" I told her. "My mom is friends with the local tourism board thanks to her job, so I'm sure we can get some great suggestions of places to shoot. Maybe we can even get some juicy insider access!"

Delaney nodded excitedly. "What if we also make it kind of like a diary, with a key and everything? To open it, you would need a 'key to the city,' just like the one they're going to give Luke," she said.

We were making progress! The creativity was really flowing — that is, until Franny and Zoey breezed by our table to sprinkle some of their signature snobbery.

"Did I hear someone say 'Luke?'" said Franny, nosing her way into the conversation. "What a coincidence! Zoey and I will be front and center at the concert next month. We also get to meet

Luke. Our dad's hooking it up." The twins never wasted a chance to hint that their dad was some rich big shot.

I exchanged a look with Ashley. Did they know about the contest yet? We didn't want them stealing our ideas. We probably had enough competition as it was. After all, there were plenty of Luke fans in this town!

"How wonderful for you," I said in a tone that let them know I thought it was anything but wonderful.

Always the peacemaker, Willow tried to lighten things up a bit. "Have you guys listened to Luke's new album yet?" she asked the twins. "It's soooo good. I love every song! It's probably his best album yet."

"Of course we did. We got an advance copy," answered Zoey. "If you're lucky, Maren, maybe we'll have Luke sign something for you when we meet him. Ta-ta for now!"

I rolled my eyes in frustration. "They are so lucky! Front and center at the concert AND they get to meet Luke? I am so jealous."

"At least we'll be there, too," Willow said.

"*And* we have our own chance to meet Luke, so take that, Prickly Pair! Concentrate, Maren," Delaney said. A grin spread across her face. "We've got a competition to win."

chapter Four

One of my favorite things about living in Valley View is that it seemed to offer the best of both worlds. Being so close to Portland, we get all the perks of a big city, but our town has tons of small-town charm.

Case in point: the so-cute-you-could-eat-it Main Street, smack-dab in the middle of Valley View. Let me try to paint you a picture: brick-paved street, really pretty antique lampposts, and a popcorn shop that has been there since before my mom was born. There are also lots of boutiques with fun names like Sew & Tell and Shoe Fly! (Fun, right?) Lots of people are always milling around, and we knew it would be the perfect place to find people to include in our scrapbook.

So before our sleepover on Friday, we headed to Main Street to get our project started. We needed to get this thing moving ASAP! The plan was to get "real" citizens to share their stories, memories, and fave things about living in Valley View — and, of course, take their pics for the scrapbook.

"Okay, chicas. Focus!" I commanded. However, Willow seemed more focused on the friendship bracelet she was braiding, and Delaney and Ash were playing fetch with Frisco and Coco. We'd figured that bringing dogs along was a good way to get people to talk with us. But right now, they were just a distraction!

As usual, I was going to have to take charge, even if it meant being a little bossy. Nothing was going to bring me down. Meeting Luke Lewis was serious business!

"We only have a few hours, so let's make sure we have everything we need," I said. The girls and I were stationed in the park across the street, trying to get everything in gear before storming Main Street. I wanted to be prepared, professional, and ready for anything.

Ashley gave me a cheesy salute. She knew I meant business! "Yes, ma'am! Maren's not messin' around."

"I never do when it comes to my future husband, Luke Lewis," I said with a smile.

I opened my backpack, which included some notebooks, pens, and my mom's digital camera. She'd let me use it on the condition that I would be *extremely* careful with it. Staying on my mom's good side was key to completing our mission! I'd also brought a few props for people to hold in the pics. For once in my life, I was totally organized and prepared.

"Who wants the paper and pen to take notes?" I asked, eager to get started.

Ashley raised her hand and smiled. "Right here, boss lady."

"Perfect! Write down everything you hear and see," I said. "And Willow, you made the sign, right?"

Willow grinned. "Even better," she sang mysteriously, pulling a pile of shirts out of her reusable tote. "I made us T-shirts." She held up one of them, which read, "I Heart Valley View — Don't You?"

Ashley looked it over approvingly. "Give this girl a bottle of puffy paint and she can do anything!" she joked. "Love 'em. Two thumbs up and five Magstars!" Ash ran her own fashion blog called "Magstar," and she loved to rate outfits — both online and off. I was always impressed by her fashion knowledge.

Once we were all suited up in our tees, it was time to put them to good use! We headed toward Main Street and picked a busy corner to set up shop. But once there, we weren't really sure how to start. The four of us just stood there staring at each other blankly. We needed to get this party started.

"Um, what now?" asked Willow. She was pretty shy, so the idea of talking to strangers was probably right up there with getting a cavity filled. It was up to me to take the lead and get this project under way.

"Follow me!" I said with fake confidence. I couldn't let my friends down. I needed to at least pretend I knew what I was doing. As fate would have it, an adorable old couple crossed the street at that exact moment. I decided to go for it.

"Hi there!" I greeted them brightly. "We're sixth graders doing a scrapbook about Valley View, and we want to include local people in it. Can we take your picture?"

The granny laughed and bent to ruffle Frisco's fur. "Are you sure you want a couple of old fogies in there?" she asked, nudging her husband.

We all laughed and nodded. This couple was too cute! "Well, in that case, count us in," she said. "I'm Dot and this is David." I handed the camera to Delaney, who got a pic of them smooching while holding up a Valley View postcard. My props were already coming in handy!

After we took a few photos, Ashley whipped out the notebook to do a little Q&A. She was a natural. After all, she had plenty of experience interviewing people for her blog! It helped that she was easy to talk to as well.

"How long have you lived in Valley View?" she asked, taking her pen out from behind her ear. (Ash loved to rock the "chic librarian" look.)

"Well, I've lived here since I was born, and Dot grew up in California," shared David. "We met at a Grateful Dead concert down in San Francisco in the late 1960s. Way before you were born. Probably way before your parents were born!"

"What's the Grateful Dead?" asked Ashley. But before David or Dot could answer, Willow chimed in.

"They were this really cool folk-rock band that had a huge hippie following until the eighties," answered Willow. "I think my parents followed them around the country in an Airstream trailer at one point."

"Right you are, little lady," said Dot. "Those were the days! Anyway, we stayed in touch by writing letters after that. David always sent me beautiful pictures of Valley View and his family's vineyard. After a while, he convinced me to move here to marry him, and the rest is history! He was quite the charmer."

David smiled and gave his wife a kiss on the cheek. "I might be able to dig up some old love letters to photocopy for you," he said. "Would you want one for the scrapbook?"

"Yes with a capital 'Y!'" I yelled. I just couldn't contain my excitement. This was too perfect! "Thank you so much."

The day kept getting better from there. We interviewed a hilarious street musician who always plays on the same corner, rain or shine (which is impressive and a little crazy), and Delaney got a fantastic pic of him with his accordion. He even let us play it!

Willow managed to lure the popcorn shop owner out to share all the stories she'd heard over the years. I shouldn't have been surprised by the amount of incredible stories she had. She was truly a town historian without even knowing it!

We also got a picture of Ashley posing on a horse with one of the policemen standing next to it. (Only Ash could get away with that!) How many towns still use police on horseback? Another reason to love Valley View.

We'd interviewed more than ten people and were about to close up shop when a friendly woman in a yoga outfit approached us. "Your dogs are so cute!" she exclaimed. "Don't you girls go to Valley View Middle?"

"Yeah, we do," answered Ashley. "How did you know?"

She smiled. "My twins, Franny and Zoey Martin, go there as well. They're in sixth grade."

"Oh, um, hi, Mrs. Martin," I managed. How was this sweet lady who seemed to be in a state of yoga Zen even remotely related to the

Prickly Pair? Maybe she'd adopted them from an evil witch or something.

Noticing our T-shirts, Mrs. Martin got curious. "What are you girls up to, anyway? Is this for a school project?"

Delaney thought quick. "Oh, um, extra credit," she said. It wasn't *totally* made up. After all, hopefully we'd get credit for all our hard work in the form of Luke Lewis love and winning the contest.

Mrs. Martin adjusted her yoga mat and gave a little wave. "Well, good luck," she wished us. "We'll have to have you girls over for lunch sometime! I'm sure my girls would just love that!"

Now *that* was about as likely to happen as us actually getting school credit for this project. It was hard to hold back the laughter after that crazy suggestion, but we somehow managed as she waved goodbye. It had been an eventful day, and even the thought of being trapped in a house with the terrible twosome couldn't bring us four down!

We made huge progress on our scrapbook Friday and Saturday, but even I couldn't have predicted how incredible Sunday was going to be.

chapter Five

Be ready at 10:00 a.m. sharp — don't be late because you've got a very important (surprise) date!

I'd gotten the cryptic Alice in Wonderland-style text from Ashley that morning as I was stuffing my face with blueberry pancakes. I immediately called Delaney to see if she had the inside scoop, but she knew nothing. All we knew was that we'd planned to take pictures around town for the scrapbook, but nothing beyond that. Knowing Ashley, she surely had something up her sleeve!

So, at 9:59 a.m., I was eagerly waiting for Ashley to arrive. Right on time, her brother Gino's clunky blue station wagon came rolling down the street. (I heard it before I saw it — that thing was definitely on its last leg!) As they pulled into the driveway, I saw something pop through the sunroof and start waving around. It was a cardboard cutout of Luke Lewis!

I burst into hysterical laughter. Cardboard or not, I was about to have an all-day date with Luke Lewis. Classic. The car stopped and Ash popped out, wearing a "Keep Portland Weird" tank top and holding up the life-sized cutout. I will never forget this moment! It was almost too amazing to even describe!

"Could you die?" she said with a big grin. "I can't believe I kept the secret this long. My shopping habit finally paid off! I convinced the record store manager to give it to me. He agreed since I spend so much time and money there."

"This is beyond amazing!" I said, still surprised. "He'll make the perfect finishing touch in all of our photos."

Gino rolled his eyes, leaning against the car. "As if it wasn't bad enough driving four girls around all day. Now I get to chauffeur a cardboard pop star. Joy."

Ashley playfully punched him. "Do you want my allowance for this month or what?" she asked. Turning toward us, she added, "He's saving up for a new car. Obviously." It sputtered a little as if to prove her point.

My mom grimaced a little. "Um, is that thing safe?" I knew she wasn't crazy about the idea of us riding around with Gino, but he'd driven us around plenty of times before with no problems.

"You know it, Mrs. T," he said. "Don't you worry about a thing."

Ashley grinned. "We better be, or no allowance for you," she joked.

At that moment, a wave of gratitude washed over me. It was pretty overwhelming to realize just how much my friends supported me, even to the point of Ash giving up her own allowance. I mean, they all wanted to win the contest, too, but this was mostly my thing. I was so lucky to have BFFs — and their cool brothers — who went the extra mile to help me out.

I gave her a giant bear hug. "Forget Luke Lewis! *You're* the rock star, Ashley Maggio," I told her. "Now let's go freak out our friends with your insanely impressive surprise."

After my mom gave us some snacks and water to take along, we were on our way. I wanted to pop a Luke Lewis CD in the stereo, but it turned out his radio only played old cassette tapes. Whoa! Major retro, but no biggie. I just played songs from my phone instead.

We got to Delaney's house just as my favorite song finished. She just happened to be outside already playing with Frisco when we pulled up.

She was equally as surprised by the cutout as I had been. We all laughed when she quipped, "Forget Frisco! *I* almost peed on the grass when I saw you guys pull up!"

Willow was jazzed, too, but she was even more excited about the secret weapons she was bringing along. One of them was an old-school camera she'd borrowed from her dad. It added cool photo effects and filters, like a real-life Instagram! She also brought along a fish-eye lens that gave a cool fishbowl look to the photos, as well as a regular digital camera. Leave it to Willow to come up with a rockin' bag of tricks!

Our first stop was the cool rainbow crosswalk at the corner of Figtree Lane and Maryland Avenue. Willow's dad had suggested we recreate the cover of the Beatles *Abbey Road* album. Willow passed it around so that we could all see how to pose.

"This is a brilliant idea!" I said. "It's a great way to tie in some music legends with both Valley View and Luke Lewis."

Delaney looked thoughtful. "Wait, who's going to take the photo?" she asked. All of us looked at Gino at the same time and then burst out laughing.

He threw his hands up in the air, but then he laughed, too. "All right, I can take a hint. Might as well make myself useful," he allowed, taking the camera from Willow. "But there is no way I'm actually going to be in any of these pictures."

"That's okay, because we didn't actually invite you to be in any of the pictures," Ashley said with a sweet smile.

"What a burn!" Gino said with a laugh.

We got some curious looks as we imitated the classic Beatles walk, especially since I was holding the cutout. We must have looked pretty strange: four young girls staging a photo shoot in the crosswalk. Ahh, the things we do for Luke! However, it was totally worth it, as the photo was crazy cool.

The park was the next place to cross off our to-do list. It has this super cool art installation with blue stick figure sculptures in different poses (like running, sitting, jumping, etc.). Gino even had the bright idea to prop the cutout up next to one of them; the rest of us posed around him hitting "rock-out" hand signals. In the dictionary next to "super cheesy?" You guessed it: us.

We visited lots of other Valley View landmarks, too, like the giant clock on Main Street and the boardwalk down by the Willamette River. In true form, the Luke cutout was the star of the show. Everywhere we went, people wanted their pic with him!

For our grand finale, we went over to the Valley View Gateway just as the sun was starting to set. There's this huge neon sign that says "Greetings From the Valley" inside an outline of Oregon. It's one of the city's "historic landmarks," and my mom had said we couldn't miss it. Our plan was to get a pic of the four of us for the final page of the scrapbook. It really couldn't be more perfect.

We huddled together on a corner across the street so we could get the whole sign into the shot. "Okay, say, 'Sleepover Girls forever!'" I prompted.

"SLEEPOVER GIRLS FOREVER!" we yelled loudly as Gino clicked the button on Willow's camera.

Soon enough, we were back in Gino's beater, and we were pretty beat ourselves after a long day. To revive and celebrate, Ashley opened up the cooler in the back, grabbed a bottle of sparkling apple cider, and hoisted it high in the air.

"A toast," she said dramatically, passing around little cups and filling them up for each of us. "This has been such a blast. Luke Lewis is going to want *our* autographs when we're done with this thing!"

"Cheers!" we yelled. Life in Valley View was good.

chapter Six

I'll give you two guesses what my fave part of the school day is. Nope, not lunch. Nope, not when the final bell rings. It's actually recess! Yep, in Valley View, recess isn't just for elementary school. It's part of some citywide movement to make students more active and get us outdoors more. Whatever the reason was, I'll take it! The less time spent in the classroom, the better, from my point of view.

And today's recess was extra important because we had a mission. The girls and I had rounded up a bunch of classmates to help out with the finishing picture for our scrapbook: a giant human "VV!"

Taking a pic at the middle school seemed to make perfect sense — after all, Luke Lewis had gone there himself. What better way to pay tribute to Luke *and* Valley View than to take a picture of a bunch of VVMS students on the playground?

Delaney and Ashley snapped into boss mode, positioning people just the right way so that the group made two giant "V" shapes. Willow and her twin, Winston, were hard at work setting up the tripod and testing the lighting settings to make sure they were right. Those two had teamwork down to a science!

Unfortunately, the same couldn't be said for some of the lame guys in our grade, who seemed determined to annoy us. They kept pushing each other and messing up the entire look of the picture.

"Hey geniuses, don't you think putting two 'V' letters together will just look like a 'W?'" yelled Chase Davis.

"Very funny," I retorted. "Did you come up with that one all by yourself?" I was so sick of his constant teasing, even if it meant he liked me. I have no interest in a boyfriend. At least Franny and Zoey weren't in our recess period. I might have had a true meltdown in that case! I was being a little dramatic, but this was really important to me.

"Can you guys knock it off?" commanded Delaney. "We've only got ten minutes left until the bell, and everyone needs to be in position."

We managed to get the photo taken, and I calmed down once Winston showed me how great it turned out. I couldn't wait to put the entire scrapbook together at Willow's sleepover this weekend.

But first I had to survive the dreaded English quiz on *Where The Red Fern Grows*. With Delaney's help, I'd managed to get through almost all of the required reading. Now it was time to see if my work had been enough! I felt nervous as Mrs. Wynne passed out the papers later that day, but I managed to make it through the entire quiz and felt pretty good about it.

The rest of the week flew by, and soon enough, it was time for our Friday sleepover. This week we were headed to Willow's house, which is always a treat. Perched high up on a hill, the back of the house is all glass and has a killer view of the whole valley. It is also an indoor-outdoor house, which means that there is a giant tree growing in the middle of it. It's beyond cool.

"Can I move in?" I jokingly asked. I threw my sleeping bag and overnight bag onto her reclaimed wood bed, then flopped onto the bed myself. "I'm chaining myself to the bed until you say yes."

Willow giggled. "Yeah, I'd swap you for Win anytime," she joked, referring to her annoying but loved twin brother.

Ash and Delaney showed up not too long after, and the sleepover was in full swing. Though I was itching to get to work on the scrapbook, we decided to blow off some steam first. After all of our hard work, a little fun was in order! Before I knew it, I was putting on a helmet in Willow's garage and hopping on a tandem bike with Delaney.

"A bicycle built for two," sang Ashley as she and Willow pedaled down the driveway alongside us. "I better not have helmet hair when we get back!"

"Who do we have to impress?" I teased her. "Willow, Delaney, and I have all seen you with crazy bed head — helmet hair can't be much worse. Plus, it's not like Grant Thompson's coming over." Ashley was crushing on Grant these days.

"Easy for you to say, curly girl. Try spending hours blowing out your hair, and then get back to me!" Ashley said. "And, actually, on the Grant note, I was thinking maybe we could do a little 'drive-by' of his house."

Drive-bys were a common occurrence during our sunset bike rides. Valley View was a pretty small town, and it wasn't hard to do a little strategic boy watching.

We flew down the street, enjoying the breeze. Before we rode down the hill, we stopped at the edge to take in the view. Ashley rang the bell on her bike, feeling free. "Hello, world!" she yelled loudly, and the valley echoed her voice back to us.

Hearing Ashley's echo was hilarious to us for some reason, and before you knew it, we were all howling and yelling random words. We probably sounded like a bunch of she-wolves! "Luuuuuuuuuke," I yelled, giggling at the way it sounded vibrating through the air.

The fun continued as we wove down Chardon Lane toward Squires Avenue — yep, you guessed it, Grant's street. And weren't we shocked when a bunch of guys from our class were playing football out in the front yard! (Usually, we managed to ride by unnoticed.)

I started pedaling faster in hopes we wouldn't have to stop, but with Ashley in tow, there was a fat chance of that happening. In fact, she was already getting off her bike and fixing her helmet hair. She is so predictable! I had no choice but to join the other girls and get off my bike as well.

"Well, if it isn't the Luke Lewis fan club," yelled Chase. "Think fast, Taylor!" He threw the Nerf football at me, which I caught with one hand.

"What else you got, Davis?" I yelled, throwing the football back at him.

"Not too bad," said Grant, who was apparently impressed with my catching skills. My dad had taught me a thing or two when he actually lived here. I'd always been so hyper as a kid — being athletic was one of the few things that kept me out of trouble.

"You sound surprised," I said with a smile. "Girls can throw and catch, too."

"I never doubted it," he said, smiling back.

Ashley, whose hair looked perfect once again, jumped into the conversation. "Oh, you're too sweet, Grant," she said, smoothing her hair.

"You girls up for some touch football?" Grant asked.

So much for riding on by, but it did kind of sound fun. The guys were up for the challenge, and even though we didn't win, I think we gave them a good run for the money.

Once the game was done it was getting pretty dark. We decided to head back toward Willow's house. Plus, we still had to work on the scrapbook! I hadn't bought all those scrapbooking tools at the store earlier for nothing. It was time to get this Luke Lewis party started!

chapter Seven

At school that Monday, I was feeling a bit like Wonder Woman. I'd gotten my grade back on my *Where The Red Fern Grows* quiz and somehow managed to score a B-minus. I was proud of myself, but I knew my mom was going to be even more impressed. Willow had also brought me the glorious completed scrapbook so that I could mail it to the radio station after school. I stored our masterpiece in my "Luke-r" for safekeeping until then.

The finished product was really something to see. For the cover, Willow had stenciled the words "I Love Valley View" in glitter paint. She'd designed it to look just like the famous "I Love NY" T-shirts — pretty cool, right? Underneath the words was a Photoshopped photo of Luke Lewis standing next to the "Welcome to Valley View" sign. Ashley's brother Roman had again put his skills to good use! I guess brothers did come in handy sometimes.

Inside the scrapbook was a collection of all the photos we'd taken — from the Main Street man-on-the-street stuff to our human version of "Valley View." We also added artsy stuff like fake picture frames, stamps, and other fun touches. Ashley has really cool handwriting, so she used a metallic pen to add captions to each photo.

And, as if all of that weren't adorable enough, our Main Street buddy David had come through on his promise and sent us some of his and Dot's old love letters to include. They were so sweet I almost cried when I read them. Talk about an amazing love story! We were really proud of how it all came together.

So imagine my supersized freak-out when I went to my locker after school and found that our work of art had gone missing. Yes, like, gone for good. Like, completely disappeared. This couldn't be happening!

My fingers flew over my phone screen as I texted Delaney in a panic. *Report to my Luke-r immediately!*

I stood there shaking as I waited for my more levelheaded friend to show up. Five minutes later she appeared, wearing her soccer practice outfit. At this point, I could barely breathe let alone talk.

"What's up?" she said, out of breath. "Coach is going to kill me if I'm late!"

I tried to fight back the panicky tears threatening to spill out. "The scrapbook," I managed. "It's gone!"

Delaney looked puzzled. "No way! How is that possible?" she asked. "It's gotta be here somewhere." She started rummaging through my admittedly messy locker, trying to see if she could find it. Her head emerged triumphantly from its depths.

"Ah-ha! This was taped to the back of your wall," she said, handing me a note.

Looks like your scrapbook is "Missing In Action." Too bad, so sad!

Unbelievable! And they'd referenced a Luke song ("Missing In Action") — salt in the wound. Delaney's face told me she felt the same way.

"How did they get in your locker? Wasn't it locked?" she asked.

I hung my head, embarrassed. "I don't usually lock it," I admitted. "It's really hard for me to remember the combo. What was I thinking? I should have had the scrapbook on lockdown."

Seeing how upset I was, Delaney took pity on me. "Yeah, but c'mon, how could you have known? I mean, who would ever steal . . . ?"

We locked eyes at the same time and blurted out our shared realization. "THE PRICKLY PAIR!"

I couldn't believe it. They had truly sunk to a new low, even for them. Those sisters weren't about to sabotage us! I shut my locker with a loud bang. "I'll handle this," I told Delaney. "You go to soccer."

She shook her head and gave me a quick hug. "Don't worry," she reassured me. "They won't get away with it! So lame."

When my mom pulled up the school driveway to pick me up, steam was practically pouring out of my ears. I was trying my best to hold it together, but I was on the verge of tears.

"Ready to head to the post office, Mare?" she said, poking her head out the window of our red Toyota Prius.

I grunted in response. "Hardly," I said, as the tears finally started pouring down my face. "The scrapbook has gone missing! I don't know what to do! The entries are supposed to be postmarked by today."

My mom put the car in park and touched my shoulder. "Okay, deep breaths," she said. "Are you sure you didn't leave it at home? Mornings are always a little crazy."

"Positive," I told her. "Mom, those mean Martin girls stole it out of my locker. I just know it! They are the worst!"

Mom frowned. "That's pretty serious to accuse someone of stealing," she said. "What makes you think they took it?"

As we drove home, I told her the whole story — how snobby they were, how they were always trying to one-up us, and how been bragging about being BFF with Luke Lewis' "people." It made perfect sense to me that they'd try to keep us from getting the same insider treatment! I don't know why my mom didn't think the same thing.

"Well, keep an open mind," my mom said as we pulled in the driveway. "That's all I ask. You wouldn't want someone accusing you of something without knowing all of the facts, would you?"

"I guess not," I said with a sigh. But as soon as I was in my bedroom, I immediately called Franny and Zoey. They weren't going to succeed at bullying us around this time. I punched the numbers into the phone and tapped my fingers on my desk impatiently.

"Martin residence," came a friendly voice on the other end. I had a feeling it was Mrs. Martin, the nice yoga lady we'd encountered last week.

"Oh, hi, Mrs. Martin, this is Maren Taylor," I said, gritting my teeth. "Are Franny and Zoey home?"

"No, they're not. They're at ballet class, honey," she said sweetly. "Can I give them a message?"

I felt *so* defeated. The post office was closing soon, and the message wouldn't matter much if I couldn't get the scrapbook back. I decided it would be better to just wait and confront them at school.

"No, that's okay," I answered, feeling down. "I'll just talk to them tomorrow."

"Sounds good," she said. "Great to see you the other day! Ta-ta for now."

As I hung up my phone, the flood of tears burst forth again. So much for meeting Luke Lewis! And not only that, but I felt like I'd totally let the other girls down. We'd spent *so* many hours putting this together, and they'd given a ton of time and energy to helping me make my dream of meeting Luke come true. (So much for my half-birthday wish!) And thanks to the Prickly Pair, it was all for nothing.

chapter Eight

Like any good mystery, things are never quite what you expect — and this one was no exception. I could never have guessed the turn of events that was about to play itself out! (Sometimes my life is just like a TV show on ABC Family, which just happens to be my favorite channel.)

I showed up at school, bleary-eyed and exhausted. I had spent way too much time last night crying. I do realize that this wasn't the end of the world, but it's hard to stop a good cry once it starts. Plus, it felt good to get it all out and start fresh.

I'd had long phone marathons with Willow, Delaney, and Ashley, all of whom had been totally understanding and tried to make me feel better. But since the deadline had already been blown, the only thing that was going to make me feel better was putting the Prickly Pair in their place!

"Are you going to confront them?" asked Willow as we walked together to history class.

I raised my eyebrows in disbelief. "Um, is the grass green?" I asked. "Of course! They may have ruined our chances at winning the contest, but they're not going to get the last word." I was way too stubborn for that!

By the time we made it to class, everyone was already in their seats and Mr. Costa was about to start. I knew I wouldn't make it the whole way through the hour, though, so once class was in session, I leaned forward and tapped Zoey on the shoulder.

"I know what you did!" I hissed into her ear.

"What are you talking about, crazy town?" she whispered, glaring at me. "I knew something was up when my mom said that you called. Delete my number from your phone, please."

"I'll delete it as soon as you give our scrapbook back," I growled. I could see Willow watching us curiously from her seat.

But before Zoey could respond any more, Mr. Costa stopped us in our tracks. "Maren and Zoey, perhaps you'd like to continue the conversation in detention?" he asked. We both shook our heads. "Then pay attention, please. We're on page 98."

After class, Zoey whirled around to finish what we'd started. "We didn't take your stupid scrapbook," she told me. "In case you didn't notice, we already *have* an in with Luke Lewis."

She flounced off in a huff, leaving me baffled and embarrassed.

And when I returned to my locker to find yet another mysterious note, I was completely confused. *You're going to give up that easily?* it read. *If you're a true Luke fan, you'll know where to find me.*

Okay, this was crazy. Ransom notes for a *scrapbook?* It was insane! I had a hard time concentrating during English class as I tried to put all of the pieces together. Was the Prickly Pair telling the truth? And if they hadn't done it, who had? And, most importantly, where was the scrapbook?

The girls and I put our heads together at lunch to find out. Ashley was full of theories, none of which seemed to make much sense.

"What if it's a Luke Lewis stalker who is trying to keep us from winning the contest?" she asked.

"How would they even know who we were or how to find us?" asked Delaney. "We're just middle school girls making a scrapbook."

"And what an awesome scrapbook it was," said Willow, who looked bummed out. She had probably put the biggest creative stamp on the project, and now all of the heart and soul she put into it wouldn't be rewarded.

Our other classmates had theories, too. At this point, the word had spread and everyone was talking about who took the scrapbook. But the one person who *always* had something to say was strangely silent. I'd fully expected Chase Davis to rub it in about the scrapbook being gone, but I hadn't seen him much today, which was really weird.

And later, I found out why. I was walking down the hall when I bumped right into him.

"Taylor!" he exclaimed. "Did you find your Luke scrapbook yet?" The way he started laughing while he said it immediately made me suspicious and mad.

"You took it!" I said. *Chase! Why hadn't I thought of that?* I gave his shoulder a little shove. "Tell me where it is! Right now! I can't believe you."

"Sorry, Taylor, that's classified information," he said. "If you really know your stuff about Luke, you'll know where to find it."

"You ruined our chances of winning the contest! You've really gone too far this time. Why can't you just leave me alone?" I said. I wasn't going to start crying, but I was super mad at him.

I started stomping off down the hallway, but he managed to catch up with me once I got around the corner.

"Wait, the deadline was yesterday?" he asked, out of breath. He seemed to feel genuinely bad. "Aww man, I feel like a huge jerk. We were just messing with you guys. I should have paid more attention. I'm sorry."

"You're sorry? That's all you can say?" I said. "We put so much work into that scrapbook. The least you can do is show me where it is, even though it's too late to do anything with it."

He agreed, and as it turned out, the scrapbook was in a locker — Luke's old locker — #241, that is. Chase and some of the guys had hidden it in there, thinking it would be a harmless joke. Wait until I told the girls about *this* one. At this point, I'd been through all of the emotions: sad, angry, frustrated, defeated. The only thing I could do at this point was move on — and *always, always* lock my locker from now on!

chapter Nine

Things in life that truly rule my world: Luke Lewis, vanilla-bacon milk shakes (try it), Broadway musicals, trips with my mom, and watching sports. And, after today, I was sure to have a brand-new addition to the list: live concerts! The day of the Luke Lewis show had *finally* arrived, and despite all the drama, Ashley, Willow, Delaney, and I were so excited to see him sing in person. Chase wasn't going to mess *this* up for us.

"You girls are going to have such a blast," said my mom, who was driving the four of us to the show. "I still remember my first concert: Michael Jackson's 'Thriller' tour. He truly was the King of Pop!"

"Mom," I groaned. "You're so old."

Ashley slapped me playfully from the backseat. "Hey! Michael Jackson's songs are awesome," she said. "And he totally rocked that sparkly one-glove look. Maybe I should bring that back." Knowing confident Ashley, it wasn't totally unthinkable. She could probably start any trend she wanted!

When we got to the Valley View Amphitheater, the outside was crazy with activity. Lots of people (well, mostly girls) were milling around excitedly, and they were playing Luke's tunes over the loudspeakers to get everyone even more pumped. It seemed like just about everyone was wearing a Luke Lewis T-shirt or holding a homemade sign. After all, it wasn't every day that a huge pop star came to Valley View!

Once inside, we snagged some sodas and soft pretzels and went to find our seats. Unfortunately, they were kind of up in the nosebleeds, but I guess you can't be picky when you get a free ticket from your best friend. Luckily, my mom had thought to bring binoculars. I guess she had learned a thing or two back in the day when she was going to Michael Jackson concerts.

Ashley borrowed the binoculars so she could survey the crowd. "OMG!" she exclaimed, squinting and leaning forward. "I think I spy the Prickly Pair in the front row!"

I snatched the binoculars out of her hand. "Gimme that," I said. "Oh, yeah, no doubt. I would recognize those blond braids anywhere."

Delaney grinned. "Well, I guess they were telling the truth!" she said. "Lucky them."

Seeing the Prickly Pair, I realized I still felt kind of bad about blaming them. Yes, they were totally annoying, but they didn't deserve to be accused of something they didn't do. Score one for Mom — she'd been right all along.

I didn't have too much time to think about it, though. The show was about to start! Flickering strobe lights danced across the crowd, and one of Luke's music videos began playing on the big screen. Then a giant "3-2-1" came across the screen and the crowd counted down as Luke walked on stage! I had never realized how loud I was capable of screaming until that moment. (Hint: really, really loud.)

Ashley grabbed my hand and we started jumping up and down together as his band started to play. It was a magical, amazing, and completely dream-worthy moment.

"I've been down the road less traveled," he sang. I immediately recognized the first line of his song "On the Run." It was hard to believe we were actually watching him sing live! A few songs in, Luke took some time to address the crowd.

"Valley View!" he yelled. "It feels good to be home." The crowd went crazy again, screaming and clapping.

"Before I sing the next song, I want to introduce someone very special," Luke said, and the audience got quiet again. "Someone who loves Valley View and isn't afraid to show it — our MOVE-FM contest winner, Valley View High School student Katie Masterson! C'mon up here, Katie."

I felt a pang of sadness as I thought about what could have been, but there was no sense in dwelling on the past. As I looked at Willow, Delaney, and Ash clapping for her, I knew they felt the same way. And once I saw Katie's project, it was obvious she deserved to win anyway. Her video started playing on the big screen as she walked onto the stage, and it was awesome. Katie had taken one of Luke's songs, "Coming Home," and put together a montage of Valley View residents lip-synching to the song.

The mayor walked onto the stage to join Luke and Katie, carrying the biggest key I'd ever seen in my life. The crowd, including myself, went crazy again! (I'd be lucky if I still had a voice tomorrow.)

"Luke Lewis, we're honored to have you back in Valley View. You've done our town proud and we hope you'll return again and again," said the mayor. "As one of our most accomplished citizens, we'd like to present you with this key to the city."

The mayor handed the key to Katie, who seemed like she was trying to keep from freaking out! She was shaking and crying. Luke accepted with a smile and gave her a kiss on the cheek! Okay, now I hated her just a *little* bit. A kiss from Luke Lewis? I would never wash my face again if that happened to me!

Willow saw my face and put her arm around me. "I wish it was you up there," she said into my ear.

"Me too," I admitted, as Luke launched into his next song, "Left of Center." "But being here with you guys is the next best thing!"

The concert went by way too fast, even though he did two encores. When he finally left the stage, we all looked at each other, bummed. Our whirlwind Luke Lewis adventure had finally come to a close. Totally tired but happy and delirious, the four of us headed back toward my mom's car. As we were walking, I felt a buzz come from my bag. I dug out my phone to find a text from . . . Franny? Weird.

Maren, meet us by Gate C. We have something for you!

I showed the other girls, who all had to do the same double take I did. Since when did Franny text me, and since when was she planning *surprises?* I couldn't handle the curiosity. Things just kept getting weirder!

"Can we go meet her, Mom?" I asked. "We'll come right back."

She nodded. "Sure, I'll go get the car and swing up to get you."

At Gate C, Franny and Zoey were waiting with their mom. "Um, hi," I said, not sure what to expect. We weren't exactly friends, so this was a little uncomfortable.

"Hey, Maren," said Zoey. "We got a little something for you at the meet and greet before the show." She reached into her leather handbag and pulled out a signed CD. A signed CD by the one and only Luke Lewis!

To Maren, it read, *Keep listening and thanks for being a fan! Yours always, Luke Lewis.*

My knees buckled a little bit as I saw my name written in Luke's handwriting, and tears welled up in my eyes as I read the message again. (I was a crying machine lately!) I wasn't sure what had possessed them, but I was *so* grateful! Maybe they weren't so prickly after all. I guess my mom was right, which wasn't easy to admit.

"Are you kidding me?" I asked, wondering if they were for real. "This is incredible! But . . ." I didn't have to say the word "why" — it was no secret that there was no love lost between us.

Franny looked a little sheepish. "Well, we owed Chase a favor, and this was it," she admitted.

Chase had talked them into it?! Maybe he wasn't so bad after all. I made a mental note to make a peace offering with him on Monday. "Plus, when our mom told us she'd seen you on Main Street and you put that whole thing together on the playground, we knew how much work you'd put into the scrapbook. We thought you guys deserved at least a little something for your hard work."

"Plus, you are the biggest Luke Lewis fan I know," said Zoey. "We figured you would appreciate this more than a normal person should."

"Wow, thank you so much," I said. "I'm really sorry I blamed you guys."

"Apology accepted," said Zoey. "I probably would have reacted the same way. So let's call a truce — for now, anyway. We can only be frenemies if sometimes we're friends, right?" She winked, but I had a feeling she wasn't kidding.

I was so excited that I couldn't help what happened next. I launched myself at both girls for a huge hug. They were surprised but not completely freaked out. In any case, I'd still take the CD and call a truce . . . for now.

If you think my Luke story ends there, you'd be wrong. I thought it was over, too, but believe it or not, there was still one more surprise in store.

chapter Ten

My mom was all smiles when she picked me up from school the next day, and I could tell she was up to something. She's terrible at hiding secrets!

"Mom, did you drink extra coffee this morning or something?" I joked. "You're acting really goofy."

My mom just laughed and shook her head. "I'm high on life. Buckle up, my dear," she said. "We're about to go on the best adventure yet."

My mind started racing. She was known for taking me out of school here and there to go on big trips with her. Were we finally going to go on the "Lord of the Rings" tour in New Zealand? Go cave diving in Mexico? Ride a Vespa through Venice? I started mentally packing my bags. Maybe I could finally finish *Where The Red Fern Grows* on the plane. That book was going to be the end of me!

But believe it or not, what my mom had up her sleeve was even better. When she pulled into the parking lot of the Marriott, my wheels started turning. Maybe a staycation right here in good ol' Valley View? I could be down for a relaxing spa day. Between the scrapbook and trying to stay on top of schoolwork, I'd been in a high state of stress for a few weeks now!

As we entered the lobby, my mom approached the front desk. "Which room is the mayor's press conference in?" she asked. We were directed to the Langley Ballroom, but before we could walk over there, my mom stopped me and put her hands on my shoulders.

"Okay, don't freak out," she warned, "but you're about to meet Luke Lewis."

I clapped my hands over my mouth to hold in my scream. "Whaaaaatttt?" I yelled, doing an involuntary tap dance. She'd managed to totally surprise me somehow. "You are the BEST MOM EVER!"

My mom grinned. "The Portland tourism board is holding a press conference and party to celebrate Luke Lewis receiving the key to the city," she explained. "I know I am gone a lot for work, but I bet you think your mom's job is pretty cool now, huh?"

I actually already thought it was pretty cool, but now it had gone up a bunch of notches in my book! "The best mom ever does indeed have the best job ever," I agreed.

Lots of reporters were gathered in the room, and when Luke walked in, all of the cameras created a storm of blinding flashes. Everyone started shouting questions at once:

"Luke, when's your new album coming out?"

"Is it true that you're dating Sara Moore?"

"What's your craziest Valley View High School memory?"

The publicist, who had kind of an annoyed look on her face, took the microphone. "One at a time, please," she reminded the reporters. "We'll call your number when it's your turn to ask a question."

I took a deep breath as I realized that I was about fifteen feet away from the man, the legend himself: *the* Luke Lewis! And this time, I didn't need any binoculars — his cute mug was right there in front of me. A quick pinch on my thigh proved that, yep, this was really happening. Eeeee!

"Want to ask a question?" my mom whispered in my ear. "I'll give you the microphone when it's my turn."

The cocoon in my stomach exploded into thousands of butterflies at the thought of asking Luke a question. "Um, okay," I said shyly. My knees started shaking, and I racked my brain trying to think of a question.

"What are some of your favorite places to go in Valley View?" asked one reporter a few rows behind us.

Luke smiled his adorable toothy grin. "Where do I start?" he asked. "I'm a huge sucker for the burgers at Tommy D's, and the Ping-Pong court at the Valley View Athletic Club is awesome. I also like to take my guitar down to the boardwalk and just relax and play."

The thought of Luke playing his guitar down on the boardwalk was like a dream. I'd have to patrol the boardwalk for the next few days while he was still in town! Can you even imagine running into Luke on the boardwalk?

I was quickly snapped back to reality when I heard Luke's publicist talking.

"Number forty-one," read the publicist. My mom nudged me as someone brought her the microphone. "Actually, my daughter's here, and she's a big Luke Lewis fan, so I thought I'd have her ask the question."

There was a collective "awww" throughout the room and it felt like *everyone* turned around to stare at me. Including Luke himself. OMG. It was now or never.

"Um," I started, forgetting what I'd wanted to say. *Pull it together, Taylor!* "My name's Maren Taylor. What gave you the idea to do the contest with the radio station?"

Luke smiled. "Well, first of all, hi Maren," he said. "Thank you so much for supporting my music! MOVE-FM was my favorite radio station when I was growing up, and I knew I didn't want to just do some regular old ticket giveaway. We worked together to come up with a fun idea that would show my love for Valley View and allow others to do the same. Did you enter the contest?"

"Well, yeah," I began, and before I knew it, I had babbled the whole story. How Delaney and I had been studying together and learned about the contest. How we'd gone all over creation taking pictures and trying to do cool, creative stuff. How the scrapbook had gone missing and turned up in his own locker of all places! Everyone in the room, including Luke, seemed pretty engrossed in the story — who would have thought a simple contest entry would have such a history?

My mom took the microphone from me. I thought she was trying to shush me, but she actually had something else in mind.

"Maren, do you want to give the scrapbook to Luke?" she asked, pulling it from her bag.

Everyone started clapping and cheering me on, and my knees went wobbly again. *Really?* I was shaking as I took the scrapbook from her and walked up to the podium.

"Here you go," I said, handing it to Luke. "I wish my friends were here to help me give it to you!"

He engulfed me in a big hug. My life was complete. "This will be great reading material on the tour bus," he said. "Thank you."

Thinking about a little piece of the Sleepover Girls on Luke's tour bus made me giddy all over again. That book *was* a piece of each of us — Delaney's determination, Willow's creativity, Ashley's outgoing personality, and, well, my obsession with Luke. It was an awesome feeling to hand it over to Luke himself! Even my wildest dreams wouldn't have matched this moment.

I'd had no idea what was in store for me when we'd started this whole contest thing, but it had turned out better than I ever could have imagined. All thanks to a little help from my friends and a surprisingly cool mom. And to think, this all started with my half birthday and the Luke Lewis concert tickets. I wonder what my real birthday will bring? I can't wait to find out!

Can't get enough Sleepover Girls?
Check out the first chapter of

The New Ashley

chapter One

"Dunzo!" I exclaimed loudly. I proudly clicked the "publish" button on my laptop and watched the newest version of my blog appear on the screen. It felt like *forever* that I'd been trying to think of the perfect slogan, and at last, I'd finally gotten just the right burst of inspiration. The tagline on my blog now said *I put the 'Ash' in Fashion.*

"It just couldn't be more perfect!" I yelled, completely giddy with excitement.

"Library voice, please," joked my friend Maren in a nasal tone, after my outburst earned a few dirty looks toward our table. I clapped my hand over my mouth as if to apologize, but not before a little giggle escaped. Maren's impressions were always dead-on, whether they were of a cranky librarian or a quirky classmate.

Willow leaned over to get a better look at my latest blog makeover. "Totally groovy," she said in approval. "I love the glitter outline on the letters, and the slogan is *so* you. Awesome."

Not to brag, but it kind of was. The bubbly font at the top of the page reads Magstar, with my new tagline in swirly font right underneath it. Next to that was a selfie pic of me wearing star-shaped sunglasses and making the standard kiss face. In case you're wondering, the blog's name is inspired by my last name (Maggio), but coming up with a fun slogan to go with it had always stumped me. At last, everything was picture perfect!

"Aren't you supposed to be studying geography?" Delaney reminded me. "This test is going to be tough."

She had a point. Midterms were right around the corner, and I was the only one who didn't have my head buried in a book. Willow was doing pre-algebra problems, Delaney was reviewing the map of Africa, and Maren was reading her copy of *Where The Red Fern Grows.* I knew I should probably buckle down, too. But it was so much more fun to bling out my blog!

"I know, I know," I replied. "But who needs geography? After all, this new blog design could really put *me* on the 'map.'"

"Ba-da-bump!" laughed Maren. "And I thought I was supposed to be the funny one of our group."

Another annoyed "*Shhh!*" came from the other side of the room. I guess some people were actually at the library to study. As for us, it was nothing new to get shushed. When the four of us were together, things got loud. Come to think of it, my life was always loud. Between my friends and my big Italian family, silence was not a common occurrence in my world.

"Maybe it's time for a break," urged Maren impatiently. She was always seeking an excuse to do something other than sit down and read.

Maren didn't have to beg us to ditch the books for a bit. We decided to go get some fresh air on the lawn outside the library. As far as I was concerned, it didn't hurt that it just *happened* to have a great view of the baseball diamond where cute guys were always practicing.

But before I could get my baseball player fix, Maren noticed a flyer on the bulletin board in the lobby.

"Yes! she said excitedly, ripping it down for a better look. "They're already starting to promote the play."

We all crowded around Maren to see what the flyer said. "Take a trip down the rabbit hole at Valley View Middle School with our fall production of *Alice in Wonderland*," read the colorful piece of paper, which was shaped like the Mad Hatter's hat.

Maren put it on top of her head like she was wearing it. "What do you think? Do I have a shot at the part?" she asked, doing a little curtsy and making a funny face.

That was a no-brainer. "I'm no casting agent, but I'd book ya in a heartbeat," I told her. "You're practically president of the drama club, anyway. You've got this one in the bag!"

Maren's face brightened. "Thanks, chica," she said. "I'm kind of the underdog as a lowly sixth-grader, but I'm still gonna bring it."

"Whatever happens, we'll celebrate your audition at the sleepover on Friday," promised Delaney. "Can you say raspberry fizz slushies?"

Just thinking about Delaney's tasty slushies made me want to fast-forward to next weekend. The only thing that beat my blog on my list of "favorite things" was our sleepovers! They had become a tradition for us four and earned us the name the "Sleepover Girls" at school. Yep, from school to studying to sleepovers, the four of us were pretty much attached at the hip — and it was amazing.

Once we got outside, Delaney and I just wanted to lie down in the grass and veg out, but Maren was still all revved up. She seemed to have one foot in Wonderland already. "You guys *have* to get involved in the play with me," she insisted. "This isn't elementary school anymore! The production value will be way better, and so will the acting."

I couldn't help but smile at her mention of our elementary school plays. Maren had starred in pretty much *all* of them, and she'd always roped us into helping out behind-the-scenes. We'd all sworn we would "retire" after last year's disastrous production of *Snow White*, but it seemed like Maren wasn't going to let that happen.

Always the artist, Willow was the first to cave in. "I guess I could help out with the scenery and props," she offered. "I bet the tea party scene would be a blast to find stuff for! "

Maren nodded in approval. "Awesome," she said. "Those giant mushrooms aren't going to build themselves. What about you, Ash? I'm sure the costume department could use some of your fashion flair."

"Thanks, Mar. I'll think about it," I said, not wanting to commit. I already had a lot going on with all my blog stuff, and I also wanted to join the sewing club at school. I didn't want to overdo it.

Just as I was about to change the subject, I saw a complete fashionista walking out of the library. Her hair was slicked back Gwen Stefani-style, and she was wearing a black sweater dress with giant hoop earrings. Who was this girl? Valley View wasn't a very big town, and we knew most of the kids our age.

And then, as she got closer, I saw "it." There is no way that was what I thought it was. I had to check it out.

"Hey!" I yelled, getting up to sprint over to the girl. "Um, sorry to bother you," I said, out of breath. "But is that one of the new Sirena Simons bags?"

The girl looked surprised. "Oh, yeah, it is," she said, shifting the bag so I could get a better look. "Gorge, right?" That was an understatement! It was a quilted leather tote with tiny skulls-

and-crossbones inside each diamond; Sirena's style was definitely impossible to miss. But the million-dollar question was: how had this girl snagged it? Everyone online was buzzing about this purse, but no one could get one.

But before I could get the inside scoop, her mom honked the horn from the parking lot. "Let's go, Sophie," she called out the window, giving me an apologetic wave. "We need to get your library card and go pick your sister up at the stables."

The girl I now knew as "Sophie" gave me a thin smile. "See ya," she said, sauntering down the path. Wistfully, I watched the bag go with her. Why hadn't I thought to snag a quick photo for Magstar? Oh well. At least my designer radar had been on target.

Which Sleepover Girl are you?

Take this fun quiz to find out if you are most like Delaney, Maren, Willow, or Ashley.

1. What kind of animal are you?
   a) a loyal Siamese cat
   b) a colorful parrot
   c) a nature-loving dolphin
   d) a tiny "purse pup"

2. What's your biggest fear in life?
   a) an "F" grade on your report card
   b) scary clowns
   c) giving a speech in front of a huge crowd
   d) a pint-sized closet

3. Which career would be the best fit for you?
   a) lawyer
   b) tour guide
   c) social worker
   d) interior designer

4. You score a trip to New York City! What's your must-do?
   a) going to the top of the Empire State Building
   b) catching a Broadway musical
   c) visiting Central Park
   d) shopping at Bloomingdale's

5. Which of these would be most likely found in your purse?
   a) a book
   b) who needs a purse?
   c) sketching pencils
   d) shiny lip gloss

6. Which social media site are you?
   a) Facebook
   b) Twitter
   c) Tumblr
   d) Instagram

7. You flip on the TV. What do you watch?
   a) Animal Planet
   b) Monday Night Football
   c) No TV for me!
   d) a chick flick

8. What's your fave sleepover activity?
   a) bike rides
   b) Truth or Dare
   c) jewelry-making
   d) spa treatments

9. Where do you fall in your family?
   a) older sibling
   b) only child
   c) I'm a twin!
   d) younger sibling

Got mostly "a" answers? You are Delaney.
Got mostly "b" answers? You are Maren.
Got mostly "c" answers? You are Willow.
Got mostly "d" answers? You are Ashley.

Want to throw a sleepover party your friends will never forget?

Let the Sleepover Girls help!
The Sleepover Girls Craft titles
are filled with easy recipes, crafts,
and other how-tos combined with
step-by-step instructions and colorful
photos that will help you throw the
best sleepover party ever! Grab all
four of the Sleepover Girls Craft titles
before your next party so you can create
unforgettable memories.

sleepover Girls crafts
Awesome
RECIPES
You Can Make and Share
sleepover Girls crafts
Colorful
CREATIONS
You Can Make and Share
sleepover Girls crafts
Fab
FASHIONS
You Can Make and Share
sleepover Girls crafts
Spa
PROJECTS
You Can Make and Share

About the Author
Jen Jones

Using her past experience as a writer for E! Online, Jen Jones has written more than forty books about celebrities, crafting, cheerleading, fashion, and just about any other obsession a girl in middle school could have – including her popular *Team Cheer!* series for Capstone. Jen lives in Los Angeles.